I0664162

INF**(N)**ITY

INFINITE POSSIBILITIES

WRITTEN BY
NACHIE CASTRO AND **BRITTANY CANDAU**

DISNEP PRESS

NEW YORK / LOS ANGELES

Copyright © 2013 Disney Enterprises, Inc.
© Disney. © Disney/Pixar. © Disney Enterprises, Inc. and Jerry Bruckheimer, Inc. The LONE RANGER property is owned by and TM & © Classic Media, Inc., an Entertainment Rights group company. Used by permission. The term Omnidroid used by permission of Lucasfilm Ltd.

All rights reserved. Published by Disney Press, an imprint of Disney Book Group. No part of this book may be reproduced or transmitted in any form or by any means, electronic or mechanical, including photocopying, recording, or by any information storage and retrieval system, without written permission from the publisher. For information, address Disney Press, 1101 Flower Street, Glendale, California 91201.

Printed in the United States of America

First Edition

1 3 5 7 9 10 8 6 4 2

G658-7729-4-13182

Library of Congress Control Number: 2013936885

ISBN 978-1-4231-9755-3

For more Disney Press fun, visit disneybooks.com.
For more Disney Infinity fun, visit infinity.disney.com.

If you purchased this book without a cover, you should be aware that this book is stolen property. It was reported as "unsold and destroyed" to the publisher, and neither the author nor the publisher has received any payment for this "stripped" book.

SUSTAINABLE
FORESTRY
INITIATIVE

Certified Chain of Custo
Promoting Sustainable Forest

www.sfiprogram.org
SFI-01415
The SFI label applies to the text stock

TABLE OF CONTENTS

THE GAME

In Disney Infinity, a spark of imagination unlocks the power to play with beloved Disney and Pixar characters as never before. When you place your Disney Infinity figures on the game base, they spring to life in the game. The more you play, the more characters, buildings, and gadgets will be unlocked for your adventures.

THE PLAY SETS

Disney Infinity comes with exciting Play Sets, where you can play with Disney and Pixar characters right in their wild, thrilling, and enchanted worlds. Whether you're racing Cars around canyons, sailing the high seas with the Pirates of the Caribbean, or creeping around the Monsters University campus, there will always be new places to discover. . . and endless fun, of course! From obstacles, puzzles, battles, and more, the Play Sets offer plenty of unique adventures and gameplay.

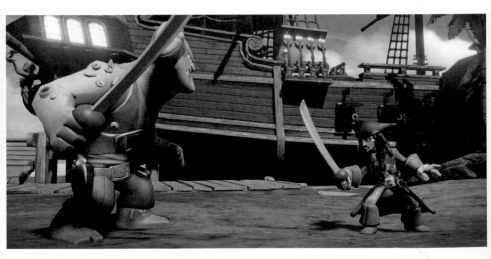

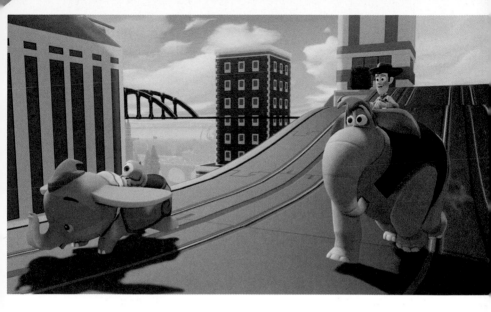

THE TOY BOX

You can let your imagination run wild in the Disney Infinity Toy Box! Bring your unlocked virtual toys from each Play Set into the Toy Box, and mix them all up to create your own game. There are no rules here—every character, vehicle, landscape, or gadget can be mashed together to make a whole new world.

Plus, you can take your Disney Infinity experience to another level with Power Discs. Simply place your disc on the game base underneath your character, and you'll unlock new powers, fun gadgets, and new ways to customize your world.

You can even share your one-of-a-kind creations with your friends. So whether you want Jack Sparrow and Jack Skellington to embark on a quest to Radiator Springs, or Rapunzel to hop in the flying Dumbo ride and race Buzz Lightyear across the sky, your story never ends!

THIS BOOK

If you're joining us on this magical journey, you . . .

A) Are ready to become a pro at Disney Infinity.

B) Want to learn more about the game.

C) Just love everything Disney and Pixar.

D) All of the above!

In any case, you are in for a fun ride exploring the beloved Disney and Pixar characters, vibrant Play Sets, and exciting Toy Box features included in the game. Plus, the game's creators have spilled their secrets on how to mash up characters and worlds in the Toy Box to create your very own Disney adventures. So what are you waiting for? As our good friend Buzz would say, it's time to blast off "to infinity and beyond!"

CHARACTERS

WOULD YOU LIKE TO BE A MONSTROUS SCARER
like Sulley? Or perhaps a Super with brute strength like Mr.
Incredible? Or maybe you'd like the sword-wielding skills of
Captain Jack Sparrow.

Fear not, Disney Infinity players—you don't have to choose!
There are dozens of Disney and Pixar characters all waiting for
your expert gaming skills. So whether you're racing around with
Mater and Holley, lassoing up a good time with Woody and
Jessie, or saving the world with Violet and Dash, you'll be having
fun. Plus, you can even get characters from different worlds to
play together in the Toy Box!

Now, as every great Disney Infinity gamer knows, the more you
know about the characters you play with, the better you'll be at
using their greatest strengths to your advantage. So let's learn
more about all the characters featured in Disney Infinity!

JAMES P. SULLIVAN (a.k.a. Sulley) comes from a long line of natural Scarers. As a young Monsters University student, Sulley was proud and overly confident, believing he didn't have to study or work hard to succeed. But after he got kicked out of the School of Scaring and was forced to team up with one-time rival Mike Wazowski, he became the kind, hardworking monster he is today. Sulley and Mike went on to become best friends and the top scaring partners at Monsters, Inc. Sulley eventually solved Monstropolis's energy crisis, by discovering that children's laughs generate more energy than their screams.

SULLEY

MIKE

MIKE WAZOWSKI'S childhood goal was to become
the greatest Scarer ever. Despite his small stature and
less-than-terrifying appearance, he studied hard to get
into the School of Scaring at Monsters University. After
an unfortunate incident resulted in Mike getting kicked
out of the program, he had to learn the importance
of teamwork. He then inspired other monster misfits
to find their hidden talents. Through this experience,
Mike became friends with former tormentor Sulley, and
eventually became his scaring partner at Monsters, Inc.
Funny and smart, Mike can achieve anything as long as
he keeps his eye on the prize!

At Monsters University, **RANDY BOGGS** was naive and timid, a particularly unfortunate combination for a Scaring major. He desperately wanted to be a top Scarer, but felt insecure about his unique camouflaging abilities. Randy wished he had self-confidence, like his roommate Mike, so that he could excel in school. Randy's number one goal was to join the best fraternity on campus, Roar Omega Roar. He'd do anything to get in with the cool crowd.

RANDY

MR. INCREDIBLE

BOB PARR, A.K.A. MR. INCREDIBLE, is the strongest Super the world has ever known! Once, he and other Supers tirelessly protected the city of Metroville, but they were forced into an early retirement. Years later, while trying to adapt to an ordinary life with his wife, Helen (Mrs. Incredible) and his three children, Violet, Dash, and Jack-Jack, Mr. Incredible was called back into action to help defeat what he thought was a dangerous Omnidroid robot. In reality, the Omnidroid was the creation of Syndrome, a former fan of Mr. Incredible who had become a super villain. Now Mr. Incredible's strength and fighting prowess are only equaled by his devotion to his family.

MRS. INCREDIBLE

HELEN PARR is the super-elastic crime fighter known as Mrs. Incredible. When she first emerged as a Super, Helen's quick-thinking and flexible fighting style made her the scourge of criminals everywhere. But after the Supers were outlawed, Helen had to hang up her mask and settle down with her husband Bob and her three kids, Violet, Dash, and baby Jack-Jack. Years later, they became the world's greatest super family: The Incredibles!

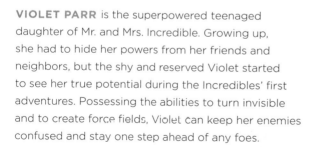

VIOLET PARR is the superpowered teenaged daughter of Mr. and Mrs. Incredible. Growing up, she had to hide her powers from her friends and neighbors, but the shy and reserved Violet started to see her true potential during the Incredibles' first adventures. Possessing the abilities to turn invisible and to create force fields, Violet can keep her enemies confused and stay one step ahead of any foes.

VIOLET

DASH

DASH PARR is the fastest kid on the planet. Mischievous, crafty, and built for speed, Dash and his sister, Violet, grew up forced to hide their talents from the world. Dash always knew he was fast, but he had a chance to really show off what he could do when he joined his sister and his mother on a dangerous mission. His boundless energy makes it hard for everyone from the bad guys to his parents to keep up with him, but Dash will always help save the day.

Growing up, Buddy Pine, the kid who would become **SYNDROME,** was Mr. Incredible's biggest fan. He didn't have any powers, so he created his own superpowered gadgets instead. But he didn't actually want to help anyone; he just wanted to impress his idol. When Mr. Incredible told Buddy he didn't need a sidekick, Buddy grew infuriated with his former idol, and dedicated his life to destroying the lives of Supers everywhere. As he grew into adulthood, he re-created himself as the most dangerous super villain of all time, using his amazing intellect to create robots, weapons, and other technology, in addition to his own super suit, complete with the powers of flight and the manipulation of zero point energy.

SYNDROME

CAPTAIN JACK SPARROW is quite possibly the best pirate anyone has ever seen. As captain of the *Black Pearl*, he's adventured his way across all of the Seven Seas and beyond, and gone toe-to-toe with all manner of foes, from the Royal Navy, to the sea monster known as the Kraken, to the cursed pirate Davy Jones, to his own former first mate, Hector Barbossa. Jack's equally at home at the helm of a ship, in the middle of a sword fight, or figuring out how to get out of a no-win situation.

CAPTAIN JACK SPARROW

BARBOSSA

BARBOSSA was once the first mate to Jack Sparrow aboard the *Black Pearl*, but Barbossa led a mutiny and stole the ship from Jack. After abandoning Jack on a deserted island, Barbossa and the crew of the *Pearl* headed off, and Barbossa was sure this was the last he was going to see of Jack. However, this was just this beginning of a series of struggles and broken alliances between the two. Whether it be Barbossa trying to free himself from an Aztec curse, or battling the Royal Navy alongside the Pirate's Brethren Court, the pirates always seem to find themselves at each other's necks. A brilliant tactician, a master swordsman, and a fan of amazing hats, Barbossa is a force to be reckoned with.

DAVY JONES

There's only one thing that every pirate fears: the monstrous **DAVY JONES.** The cursed captain of the *Flying Dutchman*, Jones endlessly ransacks ships while looking to add sailors to his cursed crew. Although he was once a man, Davy Jones is now a ruthless creature of the sea. Superhumanly strong, he also commands the Kraken, a gigantic sea-beast that can destroy ships in the blink of an eye.

LIGHTNING MCQUEEN is a world-famous race car, the celebrated number 95. He's known for winning four Piston Cups and racing around the globe in the first-ever World Grand Prix. When he's not winding his way around a track, he resides in Radiator Springs on Route 66 with his sweetheart, Sally, and his best friend, Mater. Lightning is proud to call Radiator Springs home now. Through his many high-octane adventures, Lightning has come across a few potholes and detours, helping him learn that if you have a pit crew full of friends in life, you're always a winner.

LIGHTNING MCQUEEN

She may be fresh out of the academy, but **HOLLEY SHIFTWELL** has proven to be one of the sharpest automotive spies in the business. Using a combination of her intelligence, her technical expertise, and her handy spy manual, Shiftwell can uncover even the shiftiest criminals. She can always be found with the latest spy technology, including headlight cameras, retractable wings for flight, and a holographic pop-up display. During her first top-secret field operation at the World Grand Prix, Shiftwell worked with infamous spy Finn McMissile and loveable tow truck Mater to stop the criminal masterminds behind a deadly conspiracy. Shiftwell may not be the most experienced field agent, but she makes up for this with her intellect and enthusiasm.

HOLLEY SHIFTWELL

TOW MATER (now known as Sir Tow Mater) is the rusty, loveable proprietor of Tow Mater Towing and Salvage in his beloved hometown, Radiator Springs. His favorite hobbies include storytelling and tractor tippin'. Mater values his friendships above all, often stating that he's proud of every dent he's gained on his adventures with his best friend, Lightning McQueen. Most recently, Mater left Carburetor County to accompany Lightning at the World Grand Prix. Though he may appear a bit dimwitted at times, it was his accidental venture into espionage and vast knowledge of car parts that lead him to uncover a conspiracy to sabotage the race. He was then knighted by the Queen for his efforts.

International speedster **FRANCESCO BERNOULLI** hails from Porto Corsa, Italy. As a young car, Francesco would spend his days sneaking onto the famous Monza course and racing the famous Pista di Alta Velocità bank turn with his friends. He instantly gained success as a Formula Racer champion and became Europe's top-ranked race car. Francesco recently participated in the World Grand Prix as the European favorite and Lightning McQueen's chief rival. Arrogant, smug, and often rude, Francesco's number one fan is, well, Francesco himself. Needless to say, Francesco's favorite catchphrase is "Francesco always a-win!"

FRANCESCO BERNOULLI

THE LONE RANGER

Before he became the **LONE RANGER,** John Reid was an idealistic lawyer, believing the law could solve all the wrong in the world. But everything changed for John when wanted outlaws ambushed him, his brother, and his brother's fellow rangers. As the sole survivor of the attack, John donned a mask and teamed up with the eccentric Tonto to put an end to the criminals' vicious ways. Brave and honorable, Reid learned that not everything is black and white, and that wearing a mask does not make him a bad guy. It gives him the ability to do good.

23

TONTO

TONTO is a Comanche Indian connected to the natural and spiritual worlds. He often talks to animals and seeks a way to put nature back in balance. Tonto hunts the "Windigo" or the destructive spirit residing in the outlaws that viciously harmed his people. He partnered up with the Lone Ranger to track the Windigo and seek justice once and for all. Although many consider him to be daft, Tonto is actually quite crafty and intelligent, often helping the Lone Ranger narrowly escape their many harrowing situations. Tonto is always accompanied by his black bird.

24

BUZZ LIGHTYEAR is a space ranger action figure
with adventures that are "to infinity . . . and beyond!"
For years, he had a coveted role in Andy's toy
collection, becoming best friends with Sheriff Woody
and developing a special fondness for Jessie the
cowgirl. Buzz's bravery and hand-to-hand combat
skills have helped him and the gang escape many
scary locations, including Sid's lair, Al's Toy Barn, and
the city dump. Buzz's arch nemesis (and father) is the
evil Emperor Zurg. Buzz is a stickler for the rules, and
while he can be stubborn, he is a respected leader.
Since Andy has gone to college, he has become one
of Bonnie's new toys.

BUZZ LIGHTYEAR

JESSIE

JESSIE is a fun-loving cowgirl doll with a loyal horse named Bullseye. Formerly one of Andy's toys, she currently belongs to Bonnie. Jessie is excitable, can yodel, and has a gift for playing pretend. Jessie is happiest when she feels the love of a child, and she gets claustrophobic if she's put in storage for too long. Her bravery and penchant for planning has proven useful on her many adventures with the other toys. Jessie has a special fondness for Buzz Lightyear, and a sisterly relationship with Woody, who happens to be part of the same original toy series.

SHERIFF WOODY is the wise leader of the *Toy Story* gang. He is loyal, determined, and would do anything for his friends. Through his adventures over the years, Woody has overcome his bouts of jealousy, doubt, and frustration, to grow even more courageous and clever. In fact, his plots and plans have often helped the rest of the toys achieve their goals. Woody served as Andy's favorite toy for years, and though it was difficult to say good-bye when Andy went to college, Woody is enjoying his new life as Bonnie's toy.

WOODY

JACK SKELLINGTON

Halloween Town's most beloved Pumpkin King, **JACK SKELLINGTON,** is a refined, intelligent skeleton. Every year, Jack must come up with new ideas for the Halloween festivities. Jack once grew tired of the same ghoulish traditions year after year, deciding that Halloween Town should celebrate Christmas instead, and that he should take over as "Sandy Claws." However, this holiday switch-up was short-lived, and Jack resolved his identity crisis, learning to embrace his role as the Pumpkin King. Jack loves adventure, is curious about anything new, and is happiest around his dog, Zero, and his beloved Sally. His arch nemesis is the terrifying Oogie Boogie.

RAPUNZEL was raised in a tower and hidden from the world by the overprotective Mother Gothel. When a thief named Flynn Rider stopped by her tower while on the run, she demanded that he be her guide into the outside world. But even more than seeing the outside world, Rapunzel wanted to know why, every year on her birthday, floating lanterns were released into the air. It turned out that Rapunzel was actually a princess, and that Mother Gothel had stolen the infant Rapunzel to gain the magical healing powers of Rapunzel's hair. The only tool Rapunzel needs is her 70-feet of hair, and she effortlessly uses it to get around the world.

RAPUNZEL

WRECK-IT RALPH is a heavy-handed wrecking riot with a heart. For thirty years - day in, day out, he's been doing his job as "The Bad Guy" in the arcade game Fix-It Felix Jr. But it's getting harder and harder to love his job when no one seems to like him for doing it. Suffering from a classic case of Bad-Guy fatigue and hungry for a little wreck-ognition, Ralph embarked on a wild adventure across an incredible arcade-game universe to prove that just because he's a Bad Guy, it doesn't mean he's a bad guy.

WRECK-IT RALPH

VANELLOPE VON SCHWEETZ

Known as "The Glitch", **VANELLOPE VON SCHWEETZ** is a pixelating programming mistake in the candy-coated cart-racing game Sugar Rush. With a racer's spirit embedded in her coding, Vanellope is determined to earn her place in the starting lineup amongst the other racers. Only problem: the other racers don't want her or her glitching in the game. Years of rejection have left Vanellope with a wicked sense of humor and a razor-sharp tongue. However, somewhere beneath that hard shell is a sweet center just waiting to be revealed.

PERRY THE PLATYPUS, a.k.a. Agent P, is a super-spy, part of a secret and all-animal-agent agency. With his arsenal of high-tech gadgets and his endless bag of tricks, Agent P helps keep the Tri-State Area safe from the machinations of the evil Dr. Doofenshmirtz.

AGENT P

PHINEAS FLYNN

PHINEAS FLYNN and his stepbrother **FERB FLETCHER** have been many things: astronauts, artists, super heroes, cooks, lost in time, rock stars, chased by their sister, the list goes on and on. But the one thing they have never been is bored. Not for long, anyway. Two of the most imaginative kids in the city of Danville, Phineas and Ferb spend every day of their summer vacation embarking on new adventures.

ELSA

ELSA has the magical ability to create and control ice. Although this unique talent provided her and her sister, Anna, hours of snowy entertainment as children, Elsa quickly learned the dangers behind her power. She worked hard to control it, knowing she held a lot of responsibility as the next in line to rule the kingdom of Arendelle. Intelligent, loving, and self-sacrificing, Elsa is a great sister to have in your court.

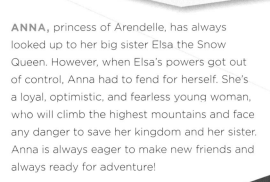

ANNA, princess of Arendelle, has always looked up to her big sister Elsa the Snow Queen. However, when Elsa's powers got out of control, Anna had to fend for herself. She's a loyal, optimistic, and fearless young woman, who will climb the highest mountains and face any danger to save her kingdom and her sister. Anna is always eager to make new friends and always ready for adventure!

ANNA

SORCERER'S APPRENTICE MICKEY

THE APPRENTICE TO A POWERFUL SORCERER,
Mickey Mouse was looking for a way to make his
chores easier. He was a bright young lad, very anxious
to learn the business. As a matter of fact, he was a
little bit too bright . . . One night, after the sorcerer Yen
Sid had gone to sleep, Mickey decided to try a little
magic on his own. Donning a powerful magical hat,
Mickey discovered the hard way that magic is both
powerful and dangerous. As always, Mickey is bright,
resourceful, inquisitive, and a bit of a troublemaker.

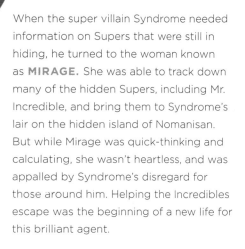

When the super villain Syndrome needed information on Supers that were still in hiding, he turned to the woman known as **MIRAGE.** She was able to track down many of the hidden Supers, including Mr. Incredible, and bring them to Syndrome's lair on the hidden island of Nomanisan. But while Mirage was quick-thinking and calculating, she wasn't heartless, and was appalled by Syndrome's disregard for those around him. Helping the Incredibles escape was the beginning of a new life for this brilliant agent.

37

MIRAGE

One woman knows the secrets of every Super, and it's the diminutive **EDNA MODE.** Responsible for the high-tech costumes and communications behind all of the Supers, Edna's lab can create anything her imagination can think of. She retired and became a fashion designer when the Supers went into hiding, but the return of Mr. Incredible and his family brought Edna's creative brilliance back. Always ready for a challenge, Edna is a Super's best friend.

EDNA MODE

JOSHAMEE GIBBS

There's only one person who knows the *Black Pearl* better than Jack Sparrow, and that person is **JOSHAMEE GIBBS**. He's served as the ship's first mate and as Jack Sparrow's right-hand man, and in doing so has seen some very, very weird things. From battling undead pirates, to fighting the Kraken, to helping to bring Jack Sparrow back from Davy Jones's Locker, Gibbs is a loyal and steadfast partner, and a steady man to have on a ship. However, possibly due to all of the supernatural events he's seen, he's also one of the most superstitious people on the planet.

PINTEL AND RAGETTI are crewmates on
the pirate ship known as the *Black Pearl*.
Originally they served under Captain Hector
Barbossa, and were members of the crew
cursed by a hidden trove of Aztec gold.

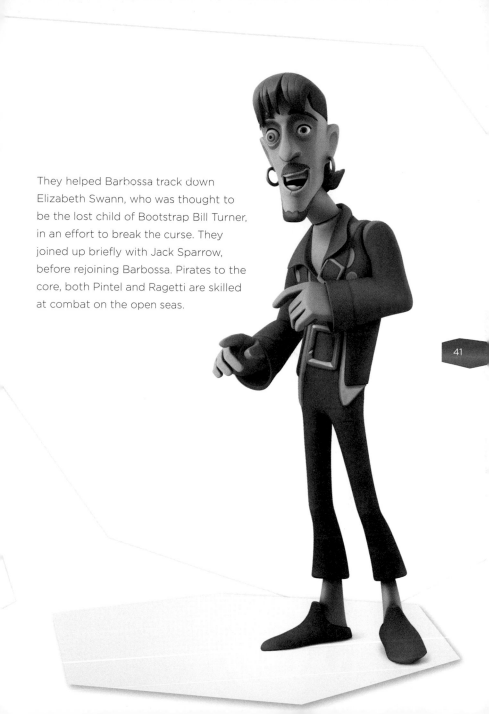

They helped Barbossa track down Elizabeth Swann, who was thought to be the lost child of Bootstrap Bill Turner, in an effort to break the curse. They joined up briefly with Jack Sparrow, before rejoining Barbossa. Pirates to the core, both Pintel and Ragetti are skilled at combat on the open seas.

41

TIA DALMA was once the goddess Calypso. Long ago, she was imprisoned in human form by the Pirate Lords, but even in this form she's a powerful magician. Tia Dalma has a deep understanding for the ways of the seas, and is responsible for much of the magic in her world. Davy Jones commanding the *Flying Dutchman*? Tia Dalma's doing. Jack Sparrow's magic compass, which leads him to the item he desires most? Tia Dalma's doing. Hector Barbossa's return from Davy Jones's Locker? Tia Dalma's doing. No matter what form she takes, she's a mischievous and tempestuous force, just like the seas themselves.

TIA DALMA

PLAY SETS

IN THE PLAY SETS, you can play with Disney and Pixar characters directly in their unique worlds!

Enroll in Monsters University with Mike and Sulley; save the citizens of Metroville with the Incredibles; have some high-octane fun in Radiator Springs; and more! Each Play Set contains tons of exciting adventures and missions, putting you right in the middle of all the action.

Now's your chance to explore all the hidden nooks and crannies of the Play Sets featured in Disney Infinity.

MONSTERS
UNIVERSITY

OKAY, FELLOW SCARERS, it's time to get initiated at Monsters U. Let's meet in the quad after class to practice our sneaking and roaring techniques. We can even test our terror-inducing skills on those Fear Tech frat guys. Fear-It Week is just around the corner, and we need to show we have what it takes to be the top monsters around!

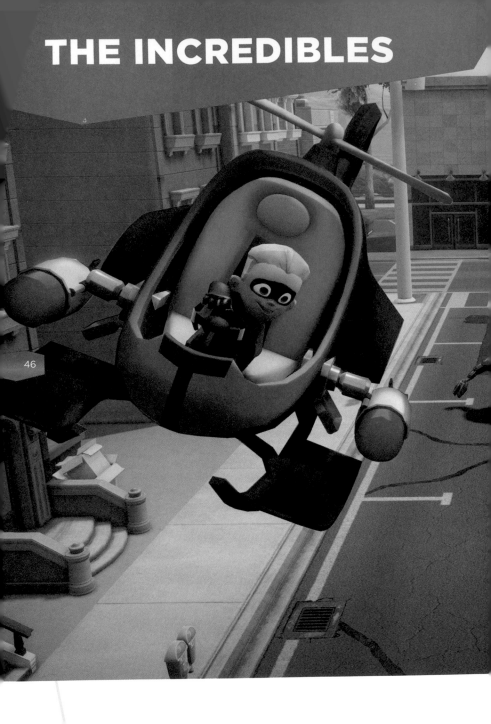

COME QUICK! Syndrome has unleashed the most destructive super villains in Metroville--and only you can stop them! It's time to use your superpowers to put out the spreading fires, defeat the Omnidroid robots, and save the citizens from the wreckage. It's all in a day's work for an Incredible family!

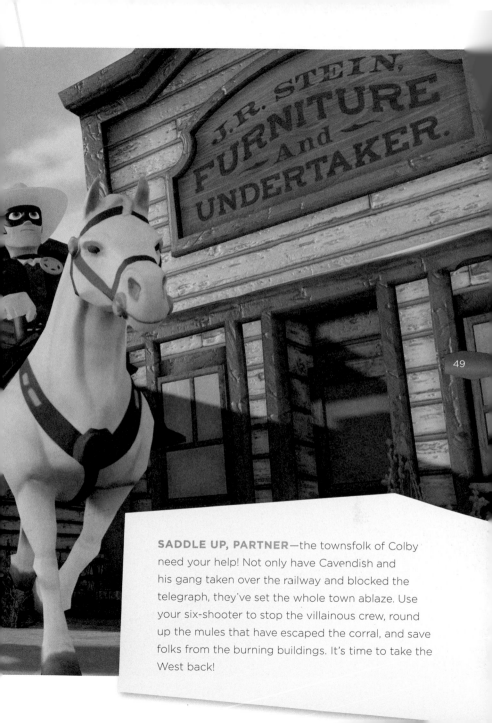

J.R. STEIN, FURNITURE and UNDERTAKER.

SADDLE UP, PARTNER—the townsfolk of Colby need your help! Not only have Cavendish and his gang taken over the railway and blocked the telegraph, they've set the whole town ablaze. Use your six-shooter to stop the villainous crew, round up the mules that have escaped the corral, and save folks from the burning buildings. It's time to take the West back!

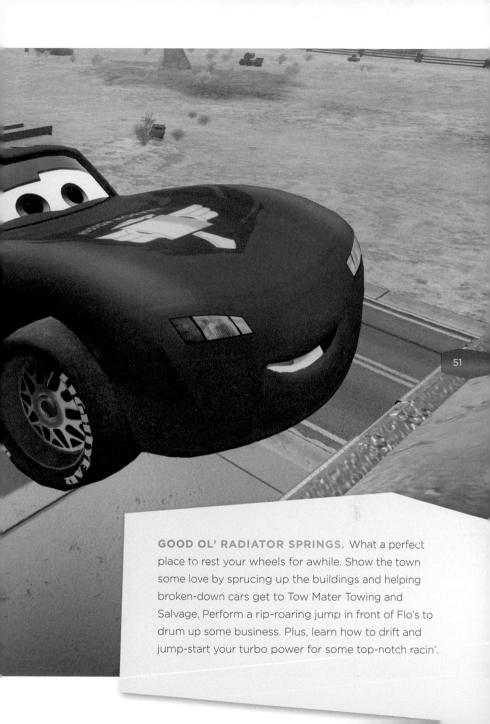

GOOD OL' RADIATOR SPRINGS. What a perfect place to rest your wheels for awhile. Show the town some love by sprucing up the buildings and helping broken-down cars get to Tow Mater Towing and Salvage. Perform a rip-roaring jump in front of Flo's to drum up some business. Plus, learn how to drift and jump-start your turbo power for some top-notch racin'.

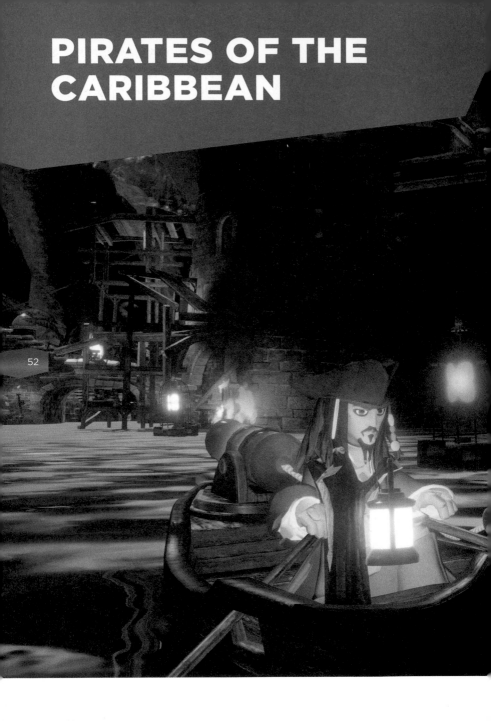

PIRATES OF THE CARIBBEAN

AHOY, MATEYS! Climb aboard this here vessel for yer adventure. Row the troubled waters to find your first mates and rescue Gibbs from his jail cell. Ward off any blackguards with your sword and pistol, and collect as many gold doubloons as you can. Just don't end up in Davy Jones's locker, because dead men tell no tales. Avast, me hearties, yo ho!

PLAYING IN THE TOY BOX

There are millions of people getting a chance to play in Disney Infinity's Toy Box, where you can mash up the unique worlds and characters to create anything you can imagine. From sports games to races, from 2-D adventures to all-out battles, anything is possible!

Want some tips on how to begin creating worlds in the Toy Box? Read on!

There were people playing in the Toy Box for months before Disney Infinity was released, and they're here to share their experiences. The following is an interview with Disney Infinity QA Testers Trevor Bennett, Carlos Rangel, and Raymond Sever, whose jobs were to tweak, twist, and

Sulley, Mr. Incredible, Mike, Captain Jack Sparrow, and Bullseye are ready for an adventure in the Toy Box!

The racers are off in the first annual Cinderella's Castle Cup Prix.

test every corner of the Toy Box. We talked with them about their inspiration, their biggest challenges, and their favorite creations in the Toy Box.

Q: WHAT HAVE YOU MOST ENJOYED CREATING IN THE TOY BOX?

RAYMOND SEVER: I loved working with the landscape elements, like the mountains and the canyons. I spent a long time creating a giant canyon that had land bridges running across it and a castle at one end. This is something that couldn't possibly exist in the real world, because physics wouldn't allow it. The ability to take it from my imagination, and not just be able to see it, but to interact with it, and even have other players interact with it, was a real thrill.

Invaders don't stand a chance against Rapunzel, her trusty frying pan, and the castle guards.

CARLOS RANGEL: I enjoyed using the *Toy Story* and *The Incredibles* elements to build large metropolitan cities. You can play with creating everything from the skyline, to the street level, down to the underground sewers. The sheer size of Toy Box is incredible.

TREVOR BENNETT: It's amazing to be able to take your favorite parts from different games and mash them all together. You're really able to customize the game for however you want to play that day. So if I want to add pieces from *Pirates of the Caribbean* to elements of *The Lone Ranger*, I can! It adds a fun factor that you don't get anywhere else.

Q: HAVE THERE BEEN IDEAS THAT DIDN'T END UP WORKING WHEN YOU TRIED THEM OUT?

RS: One of the really cool things about Disney Infinity is that it's digital. If you start something and it's not working, it's easy to delete or move things around with the press of the button. That functionality lends itself well to experimentation and trial and error. Plus, really cool things usually come out of that process. Designers or inventors seldom say, "Yep—nailed it on the first try." This game encourages people to try things out. If it doesn't work, you can just change it around. And I found that sometimes the "failure" was much more spectacular than what I had actually intended to build in the first place.

Mrs. Incredible, Jack, and Mike form a plan to reclaim the town from evil pirates.

Q: WHAT DO MOST FIRST-TIME USERS USUALLY MAKE?

CR: Definitely a racetrack. Tracks are the easiest things to put together and to understand. They're basically street pieces that you can line up and connect. And whether you create a simple high-speed loop or some ungodly roller-coaster-type track, they're usually the easiest to play with.

Q: HAVE YOU EVER REACHED THE LIMITS OF BUILDING SOMETHING, LIKE A RACETRACK?

RS: I remember the first time we jumped into a four-player Toy Box mode. We were just testing things out, so with reckless abandon, we started laying down track pieces. There were pieces that were going off of the

Lightning McQueen and Francesco face off in their new game of fire-soccer.

Uh-oh! Barbossa has found Jack's secret hideaway in Radiator Springs!

WHAT'S THAT THING JACK IS DRIVING? Why, it's a spruced-up Cinderella's coach, of course. Use the Cinderella's Coach Power Disc to spawn the princess's favorite mode of transportation in Toy Box mode.

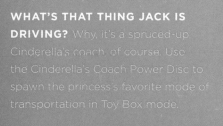

land and into the void. There were other pieces that allowed for these crazy jumps, where the cars would fall and land back on the track. Again, it didn't follow the laws of physics, and it was incredibly fun. After about five minutes, my face was hurting from laughing so hard.

TB: I think we spent more time attacking each other than actually finishing things up.

RS: That's what every game comes down to, really.

CR: You can build tracks as high and wide as you can imagine. I've created tracks that take eight minutes to run just one lap. You can even make it so that the winners get awards at the end. There's endless potential there.

Captain Jack Sparrow takes the high road over a Sugar Rush racetrack.

Q: WHAT'S THE MOST COMPLICATED THING YOU'VE BUILT SO FAR?

CR: I once put together a pretty complex dungeon. When you entered it, the doors would lock behind you. Then, you'd have to defeat various enemies before the other end of the room would open up and you could move on.

RS: I'm a big fan of pinball, so I made a giant pinball machine. I used a bowling ball as the pinball, which would launch into the table with a jet engine. The table had all kinds of obstacles that the ball could bounce off of. It was cool to realize my dream of creating a crazy pinball machine that I could walk inside of and control.

CR: And Trevor built a calculator!

Violet and Jessie ward off Zurg's robots and an Omnidroid.

Wreck-it Ralph wins the ultimate obstacle course challenge against Zurg's robots!

TB: It actually started out as a very basic concept. We created an alarm clock, and which that turned into a timer, which turned into a stopwatch. One thing led to another, and I decided I wanted to create something huge.

Also, most of my motivation came from Ray. He wanted to make a tic-tac-toe game, and I knew I had to beat him. The idea of one-upping each other has actually driven a lot of creativity. After hours of trial and error, I figured out that once you press a certain button, it will equal a certain number, and it will tell you that number. All that being said, the stuff we've done is pretty minuscule compared to what some players are bound to come up with.

RS: Trevor brings up a good point. I think you're going to see a community of Toy Box enthusiasts, who share ideas, collaborate, and push the Toy Box into places we never thought possible. Everything starts out simple and gets built upon. Eventually, it can turn into something really complex. That's the fun of it.

CR: When you start messing with the logic-based toys, ideas start snowballing very, very quickly.

RS: I think one of the key things for someone just starting out in Toy Box is not just to look at the items and say, "Okay, that's a door, and that's all it is." You're going to accomplish some really cool things by using items in ways they weren't intended to be used. You'll find that you can do a lot inside the Toy Box with them.

Dadgum! A spell has turned Mater into a monster truck, ready to race!

Sulley and Dumbo fly over the daring Disney obstacle course.

DOES THAT FLYING ELEPHANT LOOK FAMILIAR? It's everyone's favorite Dumbo ride from the Disney theme parks. Use your Dumbo Flying Elephant Ride Power Disc to generate a new, high-flying way to get around in Toy Box mode (includes plenty of trunk space).

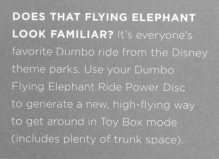

Mr. Incredible, Buzz, Davy Jones, and Sulley are ready to race.

Q: DO YOU HAVE ANY TIPS FOR PLAYERS TRYING OUT TOY BOX MODE FOR THE FIRST TIME?

TB: I'd have them look at the actual Play Set adventures. They are using the very same toys that are available to you in the Toy Box, and they all have the same names. Each character has their specific toy, and they have their logic-specific toys. Going through those different items gives you ideas. And playing the game itself, you're going to see lots of things where you'll say, "That's really cool," and you can try and recreate that and even add your own spin to it. And I think that's great. I can play through every video game that is out there, and there's always going to be something that I don't like, something where I think, "What if they had done this instead of that?" It doesn't even need to be this game—you should reference everything where you can say, "I like how this happened. Oh, but there's this one little thing that I really wish was different. So I'm going to take that part out and put my own spin on it."

But if you're looking to just jump straight into the Toy Box? I'd say play with the items. Everything and anything at first. You know, put down a door, and run into it face-first. Open it, see what happens. It's the best way to see how it works, how it's not supposed to work. Break it; find out how the world behaves before you sit down and make a plan.

Davy Jones, Mike, and Agent P try to get to the powerful amulet hidden at the top of the clock tower. The space ranger jetpack always comes in handy.

RS: And don't be afraid to start small. It can be a little intimidating because there is so much stuff, but take the time to put down a button, connect it to a cannon, and see how it interacts. Start small. Players are going to see all of these complex creations that people have made, and they're going to want to make that stuff right away. Start out small; make simple tasks. And then from those simple tasks, branch off, and you'll find things become more complex. Also, take the time to really examine the pieces. Look at something and say, "Okay, this button here, let's see if this button can interact with a car. Let's see if it can interact with a door." You'll find that the pieces can interact with each other in some really surprising ways. You're going to see a lot of cool stuff, you're going to want to make it all right away, but if you really examine and learn, you're going to master it.

Mike and Anna reach new heights during their morning exploration.

CR: My first piece of advice would be to write things down. Write down all of your ideas. It will help to remember what works well with what, what's connected to this, what's connected to that. Diagrams help you see everything at once, instead of one element at a time.

Q: CAN YOU DESCRIBE THE DISNEY INFINITY TOYS A BIT MORE?

RS: They're a set of toys that can be programmed to perform certain actions, when used in conjunction with other toys.

TB: Those are going to be your triggers, the things that can make the cause and effect happen. Almost all of the toys have something that can happen to them. For example, when I perform a trick using a specific car, I can

Sorcerer's Apprentice Mickey casts a spell to tidy up the courtyard.

Buzz and a monster truck Lightning play forest beach ball.

link it to a specific cannon to go off like it's saying, "Good job, you did a trick!" It's a category of toys that require the player's input to cause whatever you've set to be a specific output.

Q: WHAT HAVE BEEN THE INSPIRATIONS FOR YOUR FAVORITE CREATIONS?

CR: I play a lot of tabletop games, and that's where a lot of my inspiration comes from. I like to build terrain where I can imagine several people coming in and having an all-out shootout.

RS: I went through a period where I was trying to recreate scenes from famous movies in Toy Box. And I thought, "What if I built the Death Star trench scene from *Star Wars*? Then, in the middle of building a canyon, I thought, "and if I put a rope bridge across here, it'll be like the last scene from *Temple of Doom* . . ." I remember setting up the scenes, playing them out, and recording them. The other testers and I got a huge kick out of watching them over again on video.

TB: My biggest inspiration has been failure [laughs]. I hate not being able to figure something out, and instead of giving up, I try that much harder to make it work. Being able to fail a thousand times makes it really satisfying to get it right that one time. And then you get to brag about it, and which is a huge plus.

RS: Ha! That is always motivating.

TB: And the Disney Infinity storylines themselves inspire you to take a deeper look at how the programmers set

Jack gives Phineas a fencing lesson.

Can **Jack Skellington's** Astro Blasters car outrun Woody's Light Runner and the team of Mr. Incredible and Stitch?

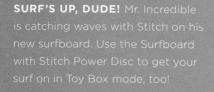

SURF'S UP, DUDE! Mr. Incredible is catching waves with Stitch on his new surfboard. Use the Surfboard with Stitch Power Disc to get your surf on in Toy Box mode, too!

things up. Once you're able to recreate those things, you start thinking, "Well, if that's what the game programmer does, and I figure out how to do the same thing they did, then I'm starting to be as good as them." That's inspirational. "Let me create something that they didn't think about. Let me be the first to create this aspect of the game that people are going to love."

CR: And it's also great to recreate your favorite games, and then to twist them around or put your favorite Disney characters in them.

Q: DO YOU HAVE FAVORITE CHARACTERS THAT YOU LIKE TO PLAY WITH?

RS: I'm a big sci-fi fan, so I really like playing with Buzz Lightyear. I like his jetpack, and he's just a really cool design, so I find myself doing sci-fi–oriented adventures with him.

Vanellope beats Francesco by a landslide.

CR: I love recreating huge cities and running around fighting the enemies as the Incredibles. It's so much fun pretending like I'm playing through stuff that's going on beyond the end of the movie.

TB: My favorite movie is *Pirates of the Caribbean* so it's a lot of fun to play with those characters. But it's also a lot of fun to play with characters in the worlds where they don't have anything to do with the storylines of the game as it is now. Rapunzel and Wreck-It Ralph are also fun ones to throw in the mix and add to the different play styles.

Dash is missing! Sulley (in Hook's ship), Jack, Buzz, Mr. Incredible, and Bullseye search for the speedy youngster.

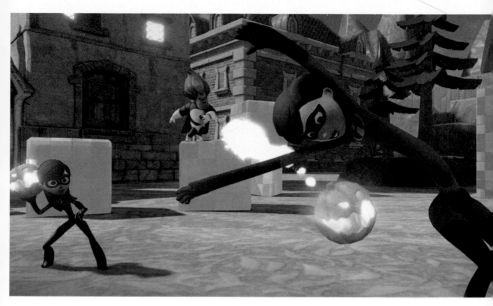

Mrs. Incredible plays a mean game of dodgeball, even when the balls are from the Headless Horseman!

AS YOU CAN SEE, the world-building environment of Toy Box mode presents endless opportunities for creativity and fun. So build the impressive floating city from your dreams; take the characters on an unforgettable quest; recreate a scene from your favorite movie. There are no rules and there are no mistakes. There are only infinite possibilities.

POWER DISCS

BOLT STRENGTH POWER DISC
This superpower disc will give you the strength to cause 10% more damage.

FIX-IT FELIX'S FIX YOU POWER DISC
Gain 20% more health with this nifty healing power disc.

C.H.R.O.M.E.'s DAMAGE CONTROL! POWER DISC
Calling all secret agents! Use this power disc to receive 10% less damage in dangerous situations.

PIRATE BOOTY POWER DISC
More doubloons, me hearties? Get this power disc to earn coins at a faster rate.

MICKEY'S JALOPY POWER DISC
Oh, boy! Take a ride in Mickey's Jalopy with this handy power disc.

ABU AS AN ELEPHANT POWER DISC
Ride in style like Prince Ali with this Abu the elephant power disc!

KHAN THE HORSE POWER DISC
Khan brings honor to us all with his speed and agility. Use the Khan the horse power disc to find him in Toy Box mode.

STITCH'S BLASTER POWER DISC
Stitch's Blaster Power Disc will take out any villains that come your way.

CANE WITH TENNIS BALLS POWER DISC
Carl from *Up* is able to get around with his handy walker. See it appear in Toy Box mode with this power disc.

POWER DISCS

SUGAR RUSH TERRAIN POWER DISC
Want to live in a candy-covered world? Use the Sugar Rush Terrain Power Disc to make the land look like Vanellope's game from *Wreck-It Ralph*.

ALICE IN WONDERLAND TERRAIN POWER DISC
Curiouser and curiouser! This power disc makes the world as whimsical as Wonderland.

FINDING NEMO SKY POWER DISC
Use this power disc to make the sky look like the sea-sational world in *Finding Nemo*.

TANGLED LANTERN SKY POWER DISC
Fill the sky with Rapunzel's beloved glowing lanterns.